Friends Forever

by Roald Kaldestad (Text)
and Bjørn Rune Lie (Illustrations)

Translated from the Norwegian by Rosie Hedger

Published by Little Gestalten, Berlin 2016
ISBN: 978-3-89955-773-2

The german edition is available under ISBN 978-3-89955-772-5.

Typeface: Minion Pro by Adobe
Printed by Optimal Media GmbH, Röbel/Müritz
Made in Germany

The Norwegian original edition *To hundre og sekstini dagar* was publis-hed by Magikon Forlag. © for the Norwegian original: Magikon Forlag, 2014. © for the English edition: Little Gestalten, an imprint of Die Gestalten Verlag GmbH & Co. KG, Berlin 2016.

The publication of this translation has been made possible through fun-ding from NORLA, Norwegian Literature Abroad.

For more information, please visit little.gestalten.com.

Bibliographic information published by the Deutsche Nationalbibliothek: The Deutsche Nationalbibliothek lists this publication in the Deutsche Nationalbibliografie; detailed bibliographic data are available online at http://dnb.d-nb.de.

This book was printed on paper certified according to the standards of the FSC®.

Roald Kaldestad
Bjørn Rune Lie

Friends Forever

LITTLE
GESTALTEN

Two hundred and sixty-nine rainy days.
He watches the leaves as they float and fall
from the trees like the pages of a calendar.
Two hundred and sixty-nine days.
And whenever it rains, he misses his best friend.

Raindrops hang suspended from the glass windowpane.
He can see all the different shades of green outside.
Brown blades of grass. Yellow leaves in the hedges. Patches of
red here and there. The central heating emits a steady hum
like an enormous purring cat. He wishes that he had a cat.
A soft, warm, long-haired cat that would curl up in his lap
and tuck its little nose under its hind leg, its closed eyes
forming two lines.

The house across the road is empty. The windows are black mirrors. He feels as if there's an empty space inside him. His father is also at home, busying himself on the computer. His parents think he has the flu, but he knows better than that. Whenever it rains, he misses her.

Everything is in motion. Drops drip. Crows flutter from tree to tree. Clouds glide by. Little birds spring up in the air from the hedges and perch on electrical wires.
—*Ding dong.*

His heart thuds in his chest. She always rang the bell, even though she knew that she could walk right in. Dad opens the door.

It's a postman with a package. He imagines her sitting by the window in her new house. Her wild, black hair. Her wide, dark eyes. Her cheeky dimples. She was his very best friend.

The package is for him—and it's from her! Inside the big box is a small bar of milk chocolate. He can't help but smile. Then he spots something taped underneath it. A letter. He unfolds the sheet of paper and lays it on the table. Written in red crayon are just two words: *yeah? yeah?*

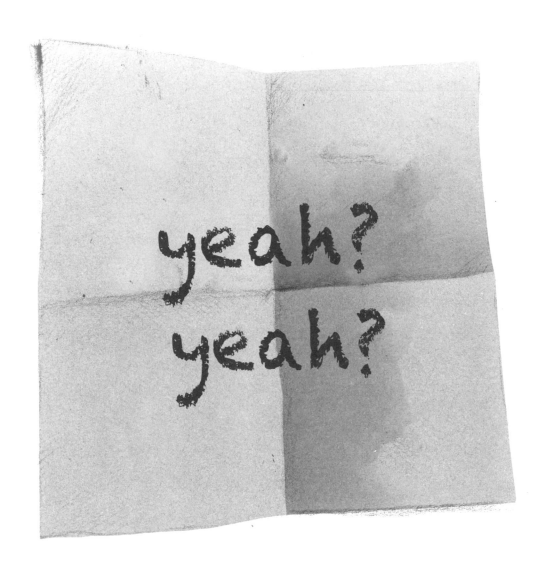

"You and Lena sitting in a tree, K-I-S-S-I-N-G."
It didn't bother them. They retreated to the forest
behind the gym where they built a fortress of pine
cones beneath the giant pine trees. She accompanied
him home every day. They jumped on the trampoline.
They climbed trees and dangled from the branches
like chimpanzees. They hopped and skipped and
laughed. There wasn't even time to eat, at least not
until they had to devour an entire loaf of bread like
two hungry wolves. Then they would sit, huddled
together on the sofa, playing games or watching films.

She slept over at his house. They giggled and
whispered in the dark, music playing quietly in
the background. The glow-in-the-dark globe shone
brightly and whirled them each into their own cotton
wool dreams.

Mom lies on the sofa watching television. Dad is away traveling again.
He calls home every evening. Mom talks quietly on the phone and laughs
a lot. He lies in bed and feels his tummy getting warm. But Dad always
comes home. And he always brings something with him, too. This time

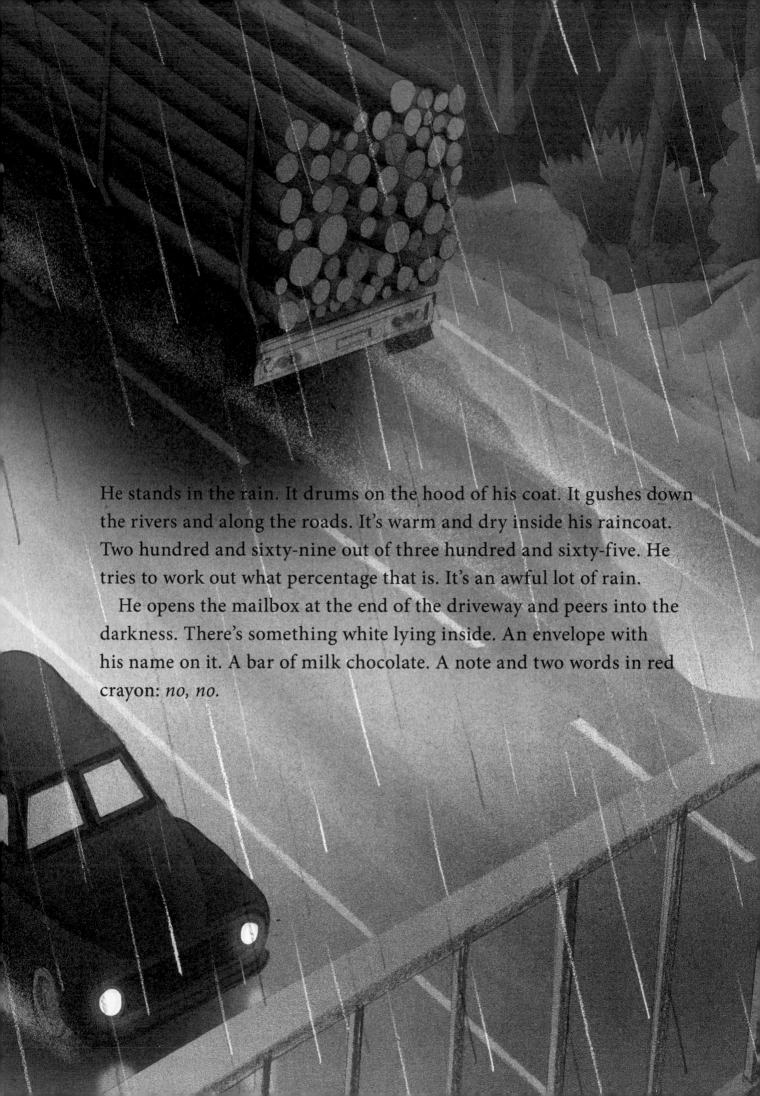

He stands in the rain. It drums on the hood of his coat. It gushes down the rivers and along the roads. It's warm and dry inside his raincoat. Two hundred and sixty-nine out of three hundred and sixty-five. He tries to work out what percentage that is. It's an awful lot of rain.

He opens the mailbox at the end of the driveway and peers into the darkness. There's something white lying inside. An envelope with his name on it. A bar of milk chocolate. A note and two words in red crayon: *no, no.*

Everything is the same. The rain has stopped, but it's there all the same—as clouds over the mountains, as mist above the treetops. The large pine tree towers above him like an old samurai. He goes out in the evening wearing his warm down jacket. He strolls along the road, kicking a pebble. He imagines that it orbiting the moon. He can hear hoarse cheering from the football field. The dazzle of the floodlights isn't quite bright enough to reach him.

He sat by this window when she left. She waved as the black car drove off down the street and disappeared around the corner. It's not as if everybody has a best friend, he thinks.

Usually the sky is gray, like Grandpa's felt slippers. Like stone. Like pencil lead. He held his pencil at an angle and colored a large section at the top of his sheet of paper. Today it's been one year since she left. Two hundred and sixty-nine rainy days.

One day, two big, tough boys blocked their way as they walked home from school. His heart fell. He wanted to run away, but he knew that they were faster than him. She walked right up to them and faced them head-on, her arms crossed in front of her chest. They looked at her, dim-witted, smirking and nudging each other. But there she stood, her feet planted firmly on the ground, her dark eyes glaring at them. In the end they gave in, shrugging their shoulders and continuing on their way. She turned around slowly and smiled. He felt his fear fade.

It was summertime, so they left the countryside and headed for the coast. She cycled without holding on to the handlebars. Her long hair streamed out behind her. He stood on dry land and dipped his toe in the water. It was ice cold. She dove right in without even holding her nose.

He stands by the playground and waves goodbye to his classmates.
He counts to two hundred and sixty-nine quietly to himself before
heading home. He takes the path through the forest, past the old
dam. At home he finds his book and makes himself comfortable
in the large armchair by the window. He really ought to have a cat
to curl up in his lap. The old lamp lights up one small room in the
big, dark house.

He listens. The house is silent. He closes his eyes. He imagines that he doesn't exist. But then Mom and Dad come crashing in, red-cheeked and bearing shopping bags. They ruffle his hair and chat and laugh, then pots and pans clatter and the kitchen fan hums, and water boils, the frying pan sizzles and the taps run.

"So how was school today?" asks Mom.

"Good."

"Good!" says Dad, smiling, giving him a pat on the back.

After dinner he goes up to his room and reads his book as the wind and rain lash against his window.

Spring showers, light rains, drizzle, summer downpours,
mist, fog, stormy cloudbursts, autumn showers.
She made the sun rise and shine within him.
She always made him feel good things would happen.

One day he spots the black car parked outside their house. He
puts on his clothes and runs across the road to their front door.
Her mother smiles at him. "Hello! It's been a while," she says.
"How are you?"

"I'm good," he says, out of breath. "Is Lena happy in the city?"
She nods and smiles.
He nods and returns to his room.

They dashed and darted through the fields. The wind whooshed through their hair. There's fire beneath my feet, she shouted. He tripped over a tuft of grass and grabbed her as he tumbled, and they rolled in a tangle before coming to a halt and lying where they landed, giggling and laughing and gasping for air. At night he dreams of a light that blinks and spins like a carousel, the two of them riding it around and around. When he wakes up he realizes what it all means. He sits up, opens the drawer in his bedside table and finds the letters. *yeah? yeah? no, no.*

He smiles. Of course. Yeah yeah, no no, yo yo. The light-up yo-yo! The same one they buried under the cherry tree. Is it still there, blinking bright in the darkness?

The sky is blue. There's not a cloud to be seen.
A yellow car is parked outside the empty house across the road. He
puts on his fez and rests his chin on the windowsill. He imagines
that he is a potted plant. A lady and a man carry boxes into the
house. Is it just the two of them? After a long while the back door
of the car opens. A girl climbs out. She's carrying a cat in her arms.
She cradles it close, gently holding it against her cheek.

He lies in bed and thinks about the yo-yo buried underground.
It's nice to think of it down there, flashing bright.

That's where it should stay.
He closes his eyes and falls asleep.